THIRST
&
FROST

JANE-REBECCA CANNARELLA

Illustrations by Jasmine Choi

Dedicated to the memories of my mean cats: George and Gula; and the basement apartment in Glenside, PA.

"There's this infomercial for sex toys on super early in the morning on Comedy Central and the way the host says 'clitoris' sounds like a dinosaur."

—Shawn Slaven

thirst & frost

Venus Flytraps

Frozen pizza is a cement stone in the microwave and my milk-breath-heavy sighs lean back in my chair—feel the sunrays of the appliance even a room away as it sings it songs of maybe-love but absolutely not because the rooms are empty except for me and the machines; and Venus flytraps came to earth by way of meteorites with their sharp teeth ready to consume and my zipper hums with the motions of up/down/up/down like you made the same sound of when you were a kid and if I could I would pluck out all my teeth and place them in the night sky like enamel beacons for sailors—but I don't think anyone is coming home to this home and my body is a widow's walk, and the microwave beeps and I can't even hand hug favorite parts of myself, so instead I eat pizza and my body bends itself into its own form of affection.

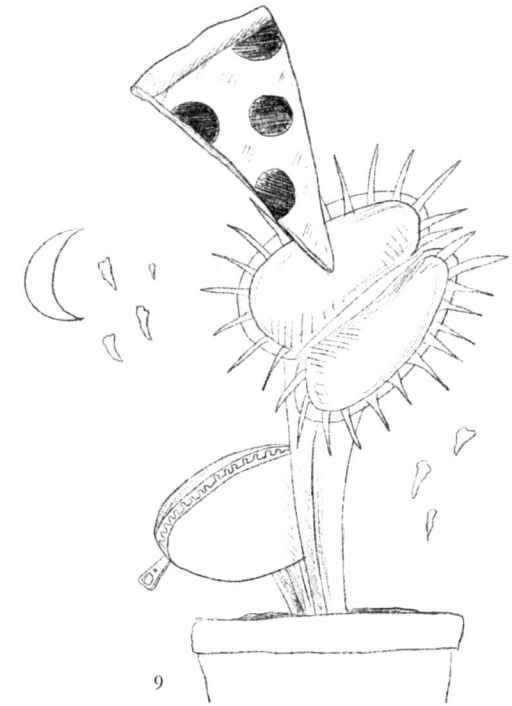

Three AM, February 26th

Three AM on February 26th is Sean who doesn't know where the moon is located because the ground is dizzy and everything is itchy like maybe his body is invaded by desert dwellers even though he's in South Philly. And I think he should do more drugs while he's obsessing over Jaybirds who roost in mysterious and unlikely places, somewhere in his chest where the heart is both an organ and a shape. The whole time he is getting batted by a sandwich with legs and eyes and ears like a cat.

If the pebbles of the universe were clusters of honeysuckle, I would take the strands of their sweet almostness and run them across my tongue and taste what time feels like: the mystery of why this night is lasting forever and filled with movement at the same time. And how one person can take up so much space that they become the actual hours of the evening. Bubbling like clouds of beer in my cheeks, Sean is fire resting on top of the Atlantic Ocean and how sometimes things feel so cold that they're actually burning. This late late February night is spun floss like twirling spaghetti on a fork with help from a spoon but still slurping up that one strand that spins against your lips; he is the whole evening with time forgetting itself until the sky turns greenish-black like a bruise and the world smells like lavender.

Sugared doughnut drugs and emotions like froth in a bath, having someone slowly soap your back and Sean is the whole fucking night as it moves in singular minutes with peaking pinhole camera light flashes in between the unsteady motion of the ground underneath us.

And if only Sean would tilt his chin, he would see that the moon was right above him all along.

Fighting Over the Best Flavor in Neapolitan Ice Cream

When I was younger, I'd spend entire days kissing a troubled boy. We'd sit in his cramped bedroom, in between piles of greying laundry, and shoot billows of white smoke into each other's mouths–clouds collecting around our heads.

I'd trace the shape of his lips and poke the groove between his nose and mouth. I think it's called a philtrum.

We'd clink spoons that made caverns in Neapolitan ice cream, listening to Patti Smith so loudly our back teeth rattled.

I wish I could remember his name – he ended up spending a lot of time kissing other girls, so eventually space and clouds of smoke erased him. But yesterday I heard *Easter* and could feel icy strawberries in the corners of my mouth where our lips used to meet.

Static

Josh eats with his fingers because when he was raised it was with too many annoying manners. He lived among dinner tables with rules like "it's rude to put your elbows near your food." Arms like bows and arrows that knocked into salt and pepper shakers. His aunt once asked if he was raised in a barn, and he said, "I wish."

So now, much older, he makes bowls of pasta and paints himself with Bengay, and gets high on brown turnpike weed, and pretends he's a robot while eating strings of spaghetti with his non-analgesic hand. In the attic like a belfry, he keeps his drum kit and even though he's old he still lives in his parents' upstairs room: a narrow-backed Quasimodo. He records himself playing music and on one track you can hear his little brother yelling "mommy says keep it the fuck down."

In the corner of his attic, under a velvet tapestry of a unicorn, is his old person's television with the dial turner and shitty reception that's hooked up to a VCR. Sometimes when he's feeling silly he watches porn on VHS tapes and turns the color on the TV to just green, and shadow, and white, and black; he says it's like watching aliens have sex.

During the night, Josh sleeps under posters from bands he liked in high school, and dreams that his thighs have turned into a mermaid's. He swims in his sleep even though there's no ocean. Under water Josh is weightless, and his fish thighs resist against the tide with sleepy undulations.

On some endless evenings with no sleep within reach, he uses ghost machines to try and see if spirits with ears like basset hounds are talking to him. He waves microphones in the air like wands, a wizard summoning specters. The recordings are waves of hisses and crackles, and Josh claims he can understand what's being said in the spaces of white noise. His friend asks, "how do you find ghosts if you never leave your room?" Josh says that the ghosts come to him; spirits that live with him in the static.

My 1st Crush is Getting Married

As a kid, I thought of you as a strawberry shortcake ice cream bar: only existing during the hottest summers of our youth. Chlorine skin, dripping brown hair, chapped lips that cracked and bled. 14-year-old fig fruit limbs ran small-sloped green hills at a swim club that we spent all hours of all days at: waded in organ-shaped pools till small sores developed on our fingers and toes. We had to close our eyes while playing water games from the hours occupied in chemicals. The girls leapt like mermaids.

One stifling mid-July day, I bounced off of almost translucent toes, red eyes shut, and dove straight into the backplates of your stegosaurus spine—chipped my front central incisor. When we got out of the water blonde-turned-green-haired Nancy said, "It looks like a mouse took a bite out of your tooth." I spent the rest of that summer with a nip out of my tooth that reminded me of you. I scraped my tongue against the sharp edges often, sanding the enamel whenever I wanted to think of that moment.

* * *

The next summer on the first day of the public pool opening – the heat so brilliant the world felt red – we dared each other to jump off the highest tier of the playground equipment. Stung our feet and shins while landing into the sandpit, it was how Lindsey broke her leg the summer before but we kept doing it anyway. In the sand, we played, "don't touch the lava," too old to play kid games but doing it anyway. The only acceptable non-lava sand was the cool, shaded, fair-haired grains under the wooden awnings we jumped off.

Having exhausted the game, you and me and a few other kids we knew seated ourselves like pretzels in the coolness of the sand; we filled our mouths with Reese's Pieces and Sour Patch Kids, and the candy would echo in kisses during rounds of Truth or Dare and Spin the Bottle, the empty green bottle of Sprite moved like a compass. Not-so-parted lips and shy lizard tongues, the kisses were like the Mortal Kombat arcade game – wasted quarters, crushed buttons – are all teens exhibitionists? The first day of summer exists in a space where time doesn't obey rules, it has always lasted as days within days – too long and not long enough, the sun a walk-the-dog yo-yo, an orange Lifesaver that never sets. As the hours passed, our summertime friends moved our seated circle to the grass and played the card game Spoons. You and I found excuses to twist limbs into each other while fighting over cards. Sunburnt skin and goosebumps the result of all hours outside – hurt red flesh, cold water droplets drying on limbs, involuntary and unknown emotions raising the quills on our bodies. Everyone sat in the sweet grasses, both in motion and not, cards in an unbroken circle, until our rides arrived to take us home.

* * *

There was a shack in between the small green hills, home of the beginning of footraces from a youthful year earlier, which sold the cool sweet treats that would melt against our summer mouths. We counted nickels and dimes from allowances we hadn't rightfully earned and swapped tastes from the bloom of each frozen flower.

The August day I turned 15, the cracks in your lips were stained blue from an Italian ice, you flipped the berry brick to reveal the ice crystals on the bottom – the sweetest part. We stood at the foot of the snack shack and looked at the slopes that led to the organ-shaped pool; the summer is an underworld with the sky made up of dew from forever damp skin. All worlds are born from chaos with no explanation.

I pulled your wrist so you would face me and in the uneven motion I dropped my ice cream bar, the bath of blue in the Italian ice cup was a spray that misted around us. Leopards spotted with candy.

Your icy tongue turned rose gold with the residue of the strawberry shortcake bar, a garden inside every person. We bumped peeling noses and having never been good at math tried to figure out symmetry and complements in the shapes of faces: sublime teen triangles, unsure isosceles. Your hands with dirt-filled fingernails rested against my watermelon-seeded shoulders, and the cold of your mouth bloomed against the hot of my sunburned lips.

* * *

Every summer is a remote in-between space where disappearance and reappearance are sprung from the blood of ice cream droplets. The melted drops flower in short-lived wounds out of shallow soil. Sea anemones blossom pink in the small hills with the summer buried and then reborn out of the green landscape; stretching pout-mouthed with slightly cracked lips becoming alive for a brief few months – a memorial to brevity.

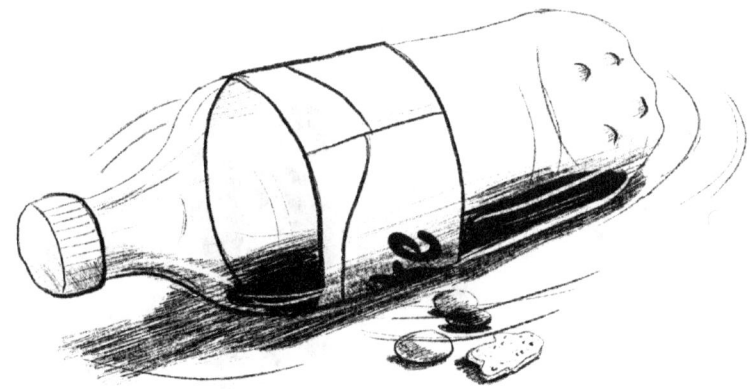

The Pool, August 2002

We fell asleep in the sun and when I woke up I was so sunburned that later on that night I got sick to my stomach. It was the summer that smelled like chlorine and cigarettes; we were staying at my parents' friends' house.

No one else we knew had a pool, and our fingers and toes became so prune-y they developed sores from too many hours in the water. "My eyes feel like they're going to bleed," you said squinting from the chemicals; they looked greener than usual.

"1, 2, 3," we would plunge under the water and shout a word; the other person had to guess the muffled sounds. On the third day you made me wear a shirt while we swam because the reflection would make my blistering skin worse.

Despite the zinc my nose began to peel and we left two days later.

In the autumn we broke back into the house to try and re-create the whole thing, but we uncovered the pool and found dirty leaves and frozen water.

A Dog's Paws Smell like Fritos

Shawn told us that a dog's paws smell like Fritos. Except he called them Dipsy Doodles, but Marie didn't know what those were because they don't have them where she grew up.

"They're like corn chips."
"Oh. You mean Fritos."

Jenny didn't believe him, though, so Shawn wrangled his miniature pinscher in order for her to get a smell.

"Actually they sorta do." And the pinscher kicked his legs.

Zack decided to look up why they'd smell that way and a website told him that some bacteria starting with the letter P was the reason. But it was normal.

Marie said that she'd never smell her dog's feet because, "that's weird."

But was it any weirder than how her friend Oliver collects wheat pennies and keeps them in a dried leather pouch on his desk? Or how Shawn's roommate Cameron only takes baths instead of showers? Or how Mike likes to eat mustard and potato chip sandwiches?

The miniature pinscher bit the air while everyone ping-ponged their weirdness around the room. Marie waffled.

"Maybe I'll smell his feet when I get home."
"Of course you will," Shawn said. "Who else do you know that has hands that smell like snacks?"

How to Break a Haymaker

During a mid-week self-defense class, concerned citizens were taught how to best remove one's self from the grip – both literally and figuratively – of danger. The man who taught the class was burly in the way that aging men in excellent shape were. Clad in black spandex shorts, muscles like softballs floated through his marine arms while he shouted moves at the class. One by one he asked the crowd to repeat the name of the person they love the most and then say: "[person's name], I'm coming home to you!" One girl said the name of her cat, but it sounded like this when shouted aloud: "Easy Mac, I'm coming home to you!" This led the class to believe that the girl's main purpose for returning home safely was easy-to-make macaroni and cheese.

The instructor wanted the group to learn how to break a haymaker – usually called a sucker punch. "Haymaker" can actually mean a lot of things: drinks, blows, farm equipment. And "suckers" are lots of things too: punches, people, candies, leeches.

The instructor said the best way to fight a haymaker was by pretending you're a robot. But how can a person tell what they're truly fighting – a fist, a leech, or sucker?

***

Maybe the way to tell the difference between sucker punches and sucker candies is by the flinches. The way a person spontaneously protects either their face or their teeth from scythe-inspired swats or boredom bites – maybe that's how you know.

According to the instructor, old time-y pugilism can be combated by becoming a machine like on Transformers and changing your arms into locomotive spikes. You'll know you're facing a sucker punch if your body changes into an android wearing boxing trunks – using a Vulcan arm against swings named for hay swathers.

Supposedly, it's easy to figure out when a coward punch is coming;

according to the instructor, it's simple to break a haymaker. But what is TRULY hard is trouncing a lollipop, though the instructor doesn't mention *that* difficulty during the class. It's the candy suckers that take you when you're vulnerable – you never know when one of those will hit.

Perhaps Blow-Pop based ennui is a product of the Charms Corporation, and fighting a corporation is hard—even if you *are* a robot. The hammer-fist shaped sucker sweetness can tuck in between your teeth, lolling against your tongue while voices like gnats vibrate the air into distraction during slow moments at work. It's not uncommon for a bored lollipop to become an unsettled loxop – it's a bird – one of those little honey creeping finches. Lollipops grow alive from dullness, and the candy finch flits against your teeth – startling you and stealing your breath.

The only way to fight an errant bird in your mouth is to trap it in a jail of teeth. But sugar beaks are strong and candy bones aren't brittle. A sudden chomp on the sweetmeat of a hard candy body can result in enamel erupting into splinters. Boredom birds born of corporation candy suckers win even in defeat.

Sometimes arms are like balers and birds are like bullets. Sickle sweep fists and treacle sweet treats are the mowing weapons that destroy calcium, and certainty, and – on occasion – robot limbs. But it's simpler to bust a boxer than it is to burst a bird.

***

The self-defense class had to let out early. During the haymaker-practice-punches one of the students got a hard candy lodged in her throat. The instructor batted the student's back while they sputtered; the bird wings of a boredom lollipop cradled in her neck. But don't worry, Easy Mac, she's coming home to you.

Water out of Wine Glasses

Home is a waterfall of lip glosses and a keychain with too many keys, half-eaten chocolate bars, and small scraps of paper with notes on them that I can no longer read – the handwriting is faded to scratches. Salt, Tabasco, and cans of Diet Coke that look like the bullets of silver-backed pounders I used to destroy from the bodega across the street from where I lived when I was twenty-eight. It was there that I once bought a pack of Kools and four Genny Creams with the change I collected from cracks in my apartment; a home like a wishing-well.

During the time I lived in the well, I had lost all my lighters and would light the menthols from the coil inside my toaster, face hovering above the lava pit. One time I singed my bangs on the hot wire and laughed so loud as I ran to the bathroom. I still managed to smoke the cigarette as I patted down my hair with damp toilet paper. Looking at my cat, orange like a terror alert, I said, "good shit, dude," and he watched while I drank the malt liquor from a coffee mug with a smug poodle on it as we both sat by the toilet.

For the brief time that I smoked Kools and lived across from the bodega and set my hair on fire, it felt like any spoken wish would be granted from the deities inside my home. And maybe that's because my wishes were modest and gods are favorable to the meek – it's a trait I've never grown out of. At least now I know how to appease apartment idols.

Since then, every home has been a bog where non-red water is a scarce commodity and I've learned to pray to the spirits for sustenance that's like food in order to stop up the hole where my fretfulness flows like a stream.

I've learned that offerings can be other human bodies sweating into ashen mattresses. When they wake in the morning I ask, "Do you know what train you need to catch?" And as their bodies retreat, gentle tides lap somewhere around my sternum. My body becomes a sacred place in carrot-top-colored dawns where springs run through me. There are coins on the carpet from clumsily discarded pants and shirts, from pockets stuffed with rattling.

Home is a graveyard of plastic bottles by the bed, single-ride subway passes, the silver tinsel from inside boxes of cigarettes – no longer menthol, and tumbleweeds of peach hair from revolving armies of beloved marbled tabby cats. Hair ties, earring backings, and wine glasses half-filled with liquid tinted red from blending water with the candy coating of wine-crust at the bottom. After god-gifts are delivered, I drink the water from the wine glass, the sacrament of the devoted, and trust that the pennies hidden in the carpet are presents from the gods for the future.

Building Bodies

This morning I touched the swarm of knots at the back of my head to confirm that we had sex last night. I was glad it happened even though I drank too much to remember anything other than you explicitly asking me for my consent and how I bit your freckled shoulder.

My hand still clutched my hair as I reached for my belongings, it was a bun made from motion and when I removed my hand it stayed in its wad. I dressed and moved out of the pillared beam nakedness of your bedroom. The paint stains were the only decoration on the grainy exposed wood and it always felt like you would get a splinter just by being inside.

When I looked in the mirror before I left, I was wrinkled and too-dry. When I was younger I didn't know that dehydrated skin looks like the creases in clothes after being pulled from a pile of laundry mountaining in the corner of a bedroom. But here we are. I am a body made of pleats. I let myself out; there was no one else to see me out, anyway, except your roommate's cats and they don't like me.

On the mud banks of the snow slush train station where I waited for my train, you sent me a text that said, "you're out of my place, right?" and I responded back "I had to fight a robot to get out but I succeeded," followed by a bunch of emojis to indicate that I was funny, and casual, and cute, when silently I was hurt that the only question was if I was out of your home. What did you think I would do? Stay? …Because in all honesty, that's what I did for a while. I slept late and held your pillows like they were bodies and it was okay that they didn't hold me back. The weight of the text asking if I had vacated like a shitty tenant carried itself deep and sunken within me as I thought about how nice the insulation of your blankets had been only a handful of moments ago.

Overly blue days that are also cold are so annoying when you're in that sort of dull emotional pain that comes with not totally being in pain, feeling feelingless. It makes the prettiness of passing bright hours feel sharp like pieces of glassy ice against sensitive teeth. The train came as my phone buzzed, and it was you again, and you texted, "you're such a cool girl. So easy breezy." And those words were loaded gunmetal grey. I'm not a girl; I'm 34.

The train showed up and glinted against the big big sky. And its hollow body housed me while we both traveled through Philadelphia, station after station, carrying me to my job in a paternal motion like a baby being rocked. The broken bodies of abandoned buildings were planted in huge unharvested rows. They had jagged window teeth like teenagers who needed braces and I loved them for their fawnish adolescent shyness, covered with ivies and with red bricks like cracked chapped lips from teeth-held bites during winter days. In the very least, I wish I could have remembered us kissing last night. But I don't. I don't think we did.

The mouths of mournful building bodies, like children not holding hands while crossing the street, became multiple-night-stand mile markers, and the train and I coasted by a station three stops before my own. I played a game that I used to when I was a teen, making bets out of probability and the universe with the too too big sky a kicked off comforter from swinging legs above me. *If he texts me again before the Fern Rock stop, he actually likes me.* And again, *if he texts me before the Jenkintown stop, he actually likes me.* But you didn't text so my phone stayed quiet, branch fingers from vulnerable trees gently clawed the windows of the train. Once more, *if he texts me before the Glenside stop, he actually likes me.* The train rocked forward and I got off at my stop.

In Case You Go Bald

When you're old or gone, I'll still be wondering about the color of your hair and how it's one color and all colors at once. Or maybe it's one color and no colors at the same time. And I'll question whether or not a person can be a pirate ship and a cruise ship simultaneously.

I wanted to learn about colors so I could develop a language for your hair, and how it falls into your eyes in the same way that boys in books that I liked were described. I don't think you "swoop" it back, but you do something with your colorless hair to get it out of your lashes that deserves to be described.

I did research but all I found was stuff about cones and rods, and your hair isn't a shape. Or maybe it's a shape that doesn't have a name yet, like that time we were walking in the rain and your hair hung in loops and lanks with bits of ice stuck in between. And how later on we made pirate hats out of newspaper and your wet hair blurred the headlines.

We examined a strand that I yanked out, pulling it taut. You asked if you could use it to tell me a joke that you had learned in 6th grade. And when you delivered the punchline, "where's the hair?" we laughed like idiots. After, having given up on colors and jokes, we lay on your furry carpet and pretended that the cracks in your popcorn ceiling were constellations. You fell asleep with your head on my shoulder.

And when you're old or gone, I'll carry the memory of how after you woke up I found elusively-colored follicles on the pillow of my shoulder and wrapped them around my fingers like rings.

Falling Toast

Like toast that falls jelly side down or the chemical compounds in effervescent streams of diet-diet drinks, you do not nourish me. Together we are plastic fast food containers that bubble out of their shape when microwaved. Intensity erodes our forms, anything contained inside us soapsuds out.
It's a sad sort of magic how food and fucking spoil in similar ways.

I identify with the strength of my hunger, eating ravenously and secretly – squirreling food and pocketing leftovers to funnel down my throat later. I eat Ma-Po tofu – numbing, aromatic, tender – with a giant spoon because I don't want to miss any flavors seeping down my throat; flames sit on top of water – chopsticks split with their fine hairs are abandoned next to me. I play, *here comes the airplane* with myself because I want to be taken care of. Talking gently to a reflection is how I practice self-care.

The me that lives in the mirror is the sort of person that spills green grass hits by over-packing the bowl, sputtering like an old jalopy. With smoke like a buckled beard, I gulp honeyed plumes of grey ribbons. After, red-eyed and fine-souled, I flow amber Vermont maple syrup directly into my mouth from a bottle in the fridge – empty except for condiment; sauces and syrups. Forever a child, I never learned sweetness in moderation. Sweetness in rivers pouring inside me until I'm fucking sick from it. Liquid flames and tributaries of sucrose fill up my body, making me dense.

***

The emptiness of you is packaged pockets of hunger that swell and rise – being buoyed by nothingness is how you float. The void is a carefree comfort – your body is inflatable.

***

On your 33rd birthday, I bought you a Mylar balloon that said, "Congrats! It's a boy!" and a key lime-flavored soda because I couldn't find the key lime pie you requested in any of the grocery stores near me.

I thought it was cute, but you weren't amused, and I ended up drinking the soda later that night somewhere away from you.

The next year, I taught myself how to bake. Made the pie. The old Mylar balloon deflated and dead stuffed in some forgotten corner of your room, we ate the tart gelatin insides and it did not embrace me – it did not delight you. Rinds in our teeth, the sour coated my tongue and I tried to spit away the citrus feelings in your sink. Leaving later that day, I felt like the balloon. Pie people, nothing between us is nutritious.

Someday shortly after, I drained packet after packet of soy sauce into a bowl since I was high and thought that there were too many in the fridge. Soy sauce made me feel something. I tried to slurry soy sauce and olive oil into a something-sauce to coat my insides, like a medicine, but the two would not marry and the soy sauce sat on top of the oil like a kiss – touching but not connecting. You grabbed the bowl while I was trying to scry the future from the tide of liquid and tossed it into the sink, magic divination works in mysterious ways. Everything escaped down the drain.

***

All throughout my childhood, my mother warned me to not open plastic polypropylene snack bags with my teeth but I never listened. As an adult, I still use my scalpel incisors to open those closed doors but it stings like lemon juice in papercuts, and I wonder what from our shared empty meals has eroded my once vampire teeth into cement gullies keeping the ocean at bay. It hurts.

This hurt causes headaches, and I swallow pills one at a time, which you said was a funny way to do it – but how do other people do it? The pills slush in the wetness of my body but heal nothing. They don't even puncture the expanse of barrenness.

Outside of your home, I watch the procession of garbage go to the trash truck and the maw of the truck eats the Mylar balloon like a doomed sea turtle. The truck breaks the colorful balloon apart with teeth that look like the ladyfingers no one wanted leftover in the beige of an office breakroom. The sun beats down on our heads while we smoke and the truck eats, and meanwhile, I just want to taste salt and hot sauce and feel the good way that whiskey-drunk and smoking feel at first. Tastes and repetitive motion fill gaps in my sternum where all the loneliness is replaced with somethingness. The truck cheerfully pulls away.

I heard somewhere that lonely Bolivian frogs are always looking for love. Buggy-eyed, I'm a frog – not particularly particular. I'm always looking for love or something that feel like the good feelings from food from my childhood: how you become full and comforted even if it's from lollipops shaped like jewelry or sour sweetness from gummies at the corner store. Maybe this is why I become attached to every stray cat that scrounges in our garbage, looking for fullness in leftovers, discards, with the hope that whatever remains in the emptiness of Tidy bags is enough.

Consider Ravioli

We're three in a row and it's warm like the way the bottom of a plate is hot and comforting after you microwave leftovers. Colleen and Sean both throw off heat to my right and my left, so much blue between both of them like the most blistering parts of a fire. And Colleen wants to know why no one will consider the plight of the ravioli. Pierogis and poptarts are pockets and appreciated. So she wants to know why I won't give ravioli another chance. *What's to hate?* We're calling them *raviolis* even though the word is already pluralized but it adds to the gentleness. My heart is all valves and pulleys, with blood sluggish in the in-between seat at the bar. Like three uneven legs on a stool, we fun-fight in a rapidly unwinding late afternoon.

Time is a fragmented line from a middle-school notebook, like how you start to write a note but then get called on to answer a question during class. Hours become skipping stunted pen strokes, and Colleen says she's going to open a ravioli stand and name it after me. A little plea for the pockets to get the grandstand they deserve. *It'll make a killing.*

Everything needs a little more sympathy and people find comfort from other people. Like the way this dude at the bar who thinks Colleen is cute comes over and we pet his wool sweater. It's warm and tender like throwing spaghetti against a wall and it sticks because it's perfect. And who am I to hold a grudge?

Nutrients are nutritious. What if I'm the disagreeable one here? The sort of disagreeable like a person yelling at you for making the meatballs wrong when all you wanted to do was cook your loved one dinner. And while I never ate the meatballs in question, I do know that they were perfect in the way that you just know something. It's the same way that bodies make their own lightning and it travels right to your sternum in shocks and surprises. That sort of knowing. Perfection doesn't go unnoticed if you actually care.

And we are three in a row. Drinking past our bedtimes on a school night, maybe we'll stay at this bar in South Philly forever? But they're running out of red wine for Colleen. So, I guess we have until the last mini-bottle, since it's the thread of time from the start of hanging out to the end. And until they cut the thread, we'll elbow lean on the glassy wood talking so fast.

I am in the pocket of warmth, and red wine is a river in the underworld pulling us all into the winter of the evening. For what it's worth, I would stay here for another six months with the three of us hothouse flowers blooming indoors during the coldest season. And throughout the frost, I could use the time left to consider the ravioli and all sorts of other things, too.

Lexical Gustatory Synesthesia

Lexical gustatory synesthesia means that all my words have tastes: emotionally charged phonemes with textures and temperatures. Like how Lisa's first kiss tasted like waxy vanilla, or that the age of thirteen was the scent of synthetic birthday cakes. And how all vacations are flavored the same; like the running water from hotel faucets, always tinged with the chlorine from a kidney shaped pool surrounded by children of businessmen.

Love is a word that can mean just about anything, the same as "nice" or "relatable." But to me it means the taste of the runny egg omelet you made me on the Monday after my job interview. It's solid in my mouth with the memory of the bits of green pepper that weren't quite cooked enough. How I didn't get the job, but you told me you loved me and it bloomed on my tongue. It shifted from the salty taste of recently cried tears that my dog licked off my face after I burned my hand, to the yolks of that overcast afternoon.

"Orange" will always taste like oranges, the same way that "sun" will always pucker like lemons. And first kisses will taste like vanilla lip gloss. But "love" will swing from a dog's affection to the taste of breakfast on a weekday night, until it eventually settles into the coppery seasoning of your jawbone – the peppery taste of your neck.

Saint Day

On New Year's Day, you suggested we celebrate by going to Taco Bell. Thirty-four years on this planet, and I had never been before. And you explained that holidays were made for new beginnings and open adventures, and we should commemorate the start of the year with something special for us to grow on. "It's rare to still be able to have firsts when you're a grown-up," you said.

The robot box was gray-metal and silver with a voice like an enraged automaton. It asked our order and I got a potato and cheese burrito. You ordered most of the rest of the menu. We sat in the blue sedan and handed off the Mountain Dew Baja Blast back and forth, it was the color of the Pacific Ocean on bright days and we traveled across the country on the wakes of the soda.

There were about eight tacos in your lap and you made me try each one. I don't remember which of the eight I like-liked, but I said they were all good. At that moment in the car, the heat on too high, I probably did think all the tacos tasted good. The ghost ships of piled ashen snow from a snowstorm two weeks prior were our only parking lot companions. You kissed my dry winter cheek, pouched like a squirrel eating too much.

"Life-changing, huh?" you said.

***

I learned about Saint Days when I was a kid in Catholic School. How the martyred devoted were venerated with a day on the calendar. Eventually, there were too many saints dying in multiples on the same day and their feasts had to be moved. Saints demoted.

The saint for my birthday is St. Roch. He is the patron saint of dogs, and the wrongly accused, and bachelors. He was often invoked against the plague.

***

After we ate, I said, "You're the patron saint of Taco Bell." And you handed me a wrapper from one of your tacos, fanned me with it before placing it in my hands. "You can worship this, like a what-did-they-call-it?"

A relic.

***

That night your hair looked like it was born from the primal murder, the freckles on your cheeks were berries colored like drops of blood and I touched my wet lips to each spot. So much red in one room. You mapped my body with your teeth fashioning craters of purple moons and storms of planets, entire universes in and on my frame. But having sex with you was always like putting my lips to water and not being able to drink. Thankfully, the ocean from earlier slaked an un-relievable thirst.

***

Your departure was a myth of origin. Our life was the persistent rolling boil of water in the pot until it foamed and spilled its tides into the flame below. I marked the time we spent together in meals: communions marked by new experiences versus those eaten in silence.

We were both stone statues. Your deadweight leg always on top of me and the blood berries I once kissed were each a stinging star behind my closed lids. Every thirst-filled evening was the same, I lived with the dryness and my life felt like the sound of a scream.

Why does devotion sometimes feel like a sickness?

***

On the day you disappeared, you gathered your stuff in garbage bags and said goodbye only to our dog. "Don't let her give you too many treats," you said petting the shaggy dog with her triangle ears. As the door closed, I became soft feathers stuck on the sticky ground outside of the 46th street subway stop. So grounded that I was pulverized. The dog kept wagging her tail.

***

A few short months later it was New Year's Day, and I was the first girl in the history of the world to be able to fly on paper wings made from the fabric of a taco holder; a relic found on its Saint Day.

The ocean is diamond-topped and hurting when you dive drop into it, but walking past the window of the drive-thru, the swells of the soda I cradled were the gentle pitches of low tide. The bag of tacos swung like a pendulum. And affection is a flower-body pressed between scraps of whatever paper you can find – preserved in its moment; the empty parking lot a whole world that existed inside and outside of me.

Lodestar, South Carolina

We can't see anything through the moss; the nighttime makes cobwebs of the trees as the golf cart gets heaved slowly by the force of our drunken trajectory. Pete tries to explain where we're taking the stalled cart as we haul it like oxen at a tumbril.

As we enter a clearing, free from the lichen, stars make puncture marks in the blackness and Pete becomes our astro-navigator. He pretends to read celestial bodies that to my blurry eyes look like specks of dust. "Not far now, not far now," he responds to our vocal belly aching. He uses astronomical terms to encourage us. The words sound like music, and poetry, and jokes all at once: polestar and penumbra and nadir and nebulous. When he gets to "gibbous," I'm red-faced and giddy with laughter.

With spaghetti arms we push the cart to the roadside, resting and sweating, while Pete repeats that we're almost there.

The Washing Machine Sang

All of the appliances in Jen's apartment sang. In her grown-up home with central air and functioning gadgets, she'd asked me to watch her mature cat – mature as in mellow, not aged – while she was away on a trip, like the ones actual adults take. "A mini getaway."

It was the day after her departure. As the sun changed the sky into soapsuds of color, the washing machine glittered upon start, spin cycle, and finish. A jaunty sweet song like the plastic teeth of a Fisher Price record bleated at the end. Matt and I had been watching a TV show about magicians and were startled out of a static reverie. Matt ran a hand through his long dark hair and said the machine was probably singing the song of its father, which sounded very theatrical.

I'm going to put the songs of washing machine forefathers on a playlist, or at least put the task of making this playlist on my radar – just like how paying my loans is on my radar, and not taking every single emotion so seriously is on my radar, like how getting quarters to take my laundry to the laundromat on 43rd and Chestnut is always on my radar.

While the washing machine sang, I turned the sound up on the TV to drown out the lullaby. I ran my own hand through Matt's dark hair.

My appliances don't sing, but I don't have any modern-ish appliances to begin with – not even a microwave. People always ask how I live without a microwave. I say something cavalier about using the oven, but really I just eat food that is cold or raw. I don't care – I honestly don't care – until sometimes I *do*, like when I'm staying at Jen's and everything is merry and melodious. Even her microwave twinkled music as I made ready-to-eat chocolate mousse from a powder packet I found in her cupboards along with her leftover milk – not even past its expiration date. I marveled at the microwave's friendliness. My envy is not contained in small ways, it is the flow of the chocolate-y pudding under a silver skin that forms on top after staying out too long.

Throughout my stay, I drank all of the vodka in the freezer. The refrigerator beeped because I kept the door open too long, pouring from the bottle into my mouth, glugging like a fish. In the freezer, there was an ice cube tray she'd bought that didn't just come with the place. I have never thought to do that. Buy an ice cube tray. Hers was rubber and blue, and the ice popped out easily, and I envied that too.

**

A day earlier, before she left, Jen had bought us cheesesteaks and cheese fries and we'd drank too much. Jen put away the leftovers but chucked the fries because "fries aren't good reheated." The next day, with her gone, I lay in her bed in my underwear watching reality TV on my phone. I ate the cheese fries with my snail fingers, having fished them out of the garbage. Matt said he couldn't show up until later, so I waited. Sometimes I called, "pss-pss-pss" for her cat to come out and join me, but he never did. He never even made a sound.

The only things that make noise in Jen's home are the robots.

**

Then later, Matt came over, and there was the music of the appliances. And we had pizza, and new fries, and magicians on TV, and really bad sex. We tried our best, but he wasn't hard. We attempted to do it anyway with limited success. And when it was all over, I apologized, and he left, and I took out the load of laundry from earlier and replaced it with the soiled sheets. I cleaned the apartment. The washing machine happily launched into a song to announce that the sheets were clean. I thought about Matt's joke from earlier, about the washing machine's father's song and it made me angry. Where do we learn how to commit to pain? It's pointless to kick a washing machine because it doesn't get your hurt — it's too busy making music to feel anything.

**

I wondered who has loved just like this before in Jen's grownup space. With computers as companions and even a faucet that chimes - are all trysts here mechanical? Or do hers turn out better than mine? Does love look better when you're an adult who has their shit together?

I pulled the sheets out: a blue piped one, a bird patterned one, the white pillowcases where, earlier, I'd found a long strand of Matt's dark hair and felt like even that feathering touch made the entire pillow unclean. I assume Jen's love is more meaningful, made under the watchful eyes of tender electronics. The bodies she invites into her home power down to melodies of automata, consecrated with the sweat of responsibility.

Then, since there was no machine for folding laundry, I became the robot. And since I was the robot, I felt like I should sing. I hummed while collapsing the bedding into pleats, while fitting fresh blue sheets onto the mattress. Jen would be home in two days and then I'd be back in my non-harmonious, appliance-less shithole of an apartment.

I never could find her fucking cat anywhere.

I Wanted Us to be French Impressionists

I wanted us to be French Impressionists, so I emptied out a liter of seltzer and filled it with $10 red wine. The bristles of the paint brushes that I put in my bag were fanned by the time we met at the abandoned Life Insurance building. We sat on the floor of a rotted wood gazebo and took pulls of sour wine, brushing hands passing back and forth.

Mosquitoes bit our bare legs while we made up stories about the building, and the tales ate up the waning day. I kept meaning to paint using the wine, but I got distracted trying to find excuses to touch you.

Security guards made their rounds and we ducked out of view, moving our bodies closer together than necessary. We agreed to leave our sanctuary, the rest of the wine having turned into red mustaches. "Let's go to the bar."

Wobbling down the street, we bumped into one another. "Look at that cat." I tripped at the sound of your voice, and the cat darted in the other direction. By the time we made it to the bar our hands found their way into one another. We sucked on Jolly Ranchers. We drained bottles of beer.

Drunk and uncaring I pulled your face to mine. Or you pulled my face to yours. Or we met in the middle. A band stopped their set to tell us to keep it PG. I laughed against your lips but didn't stop.

You tasted like fruit punch and beer while I searched the recesses of your mouth, candy punctuated breathing.

The room was hot and spinning. I rested my forehead against your chin, your hand on the back of my neck. I wanted to paint us in that moment like the French Impressionists might: openly composed, visible strokes, and full of movement.

Muskmelons

Days are the rind of a cantaloupe, and my brain becomes the sweetness of the fruit trying to find meaning in Jason's mesh patterns, the tender in the ridged and webbed design of his orange anger. To like him better, on a Sunday in October spent with football and pony-necked bottles of beer, our faces coated in seafoam, I recast him as a resin action figure. Calluses on his hands were the indented parishioners to the church of his body. Jason was a magician with worshippers of magic netted on his skin so I could forgive the bow of a mouth as it bent into a familiar pout.

Sometimes Jason and I argue about whether or not we're having arguments. Both aware that there's no room for discussing certain things, but then we do it anyway; catty teen girls who don't like who they like. Fights are map-less and route-less, and everyone is a passenger in a driver-less car. And sometimes I ask if we can take a break from the zig-zagging disputes, which ensures the battle will last another day. Two days. I guess it's a memo to make sure I never mention disliking Nirvana again.

***

That football day we fought fights about music and then men in movies who I thought were handsome. Bulls stuck in a cycle and angry knotted bodies sitting across from one another in a cramped bedroom, touchdowns screamed from the TV. At least someone was winning something.

To escape the labyrinth, Jason asked me to read his tarot cards, a gift given to me from some witches. "Let's see what they say." I've never known the meaning of the Rider Waitt and I forever made up implications for each of the passes and positions. Mean futures in shadowy illustrations, Jason and his outcomes were always bleak. The cards acted as a mouthpiece and the future read the same as always. The TV announced the 4th down. He threw an empty bottle on the floor but at least it didn't bother to break this time.

***

Since cards failed to impress, he asked me to read his palms, a trick I'd learned in order to gently touch strange men in bars. Something I once did to Jason while we were drunk at the Kite and Crow, blowing on his hands to "raise the lines of his palm."

I held the hand near my face and inspected the grooves of the palm and the yellow-y arches of hardened skin, a maze of muskmelon peel. The rootstocks of those melons were among the very first goods traveling the ancient world. Cruelty is historically inherited. For a brief moment I entertained the thought of spitting into the open hand whose hurts I knew so well.

**

As we knelt, now on the floor, a sea of Miller High Life the swells around us, his hair dipped over one eye – a vulnerable little kid, recast hero to tender child, I couldn't bring myself to say any more about his future. Sometimes sweetness is buried and the hidden tastes are treasures because they were denied. But sometimes when you find the sweet it masks the mildew, and anyway, when you think about it, really think about, melons are the worst part of fruit salads.

In the fortune telling stillness, the team he didn't want to win won. The day was all loss and my throat became a closed fist. The hollow bottles of all the beer an extension of the emptiness inside and instead of soothsaying I used the figures of the Millers to plot a chart for my exodus.
Divination was unnecessary, I never liked melons to begin with.

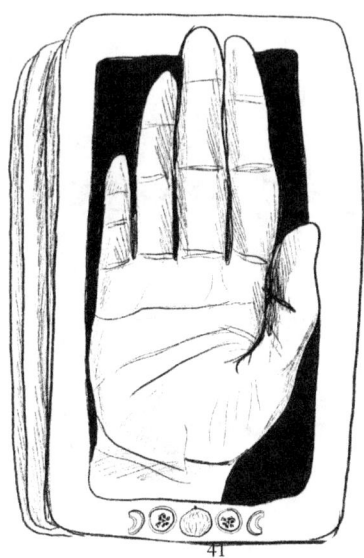

Julian, CA

On the drive up to Julian we decided to smoke poorly rolled joints so that the town's pies would taste better. "If that's even possible," you said exhaling smoke. The car windows sweated while we passed it back and forth. "It looks like a canoe," I said, meaning the joint. You nodded while staring out the front window.

Your beard looked crinkly and I reached out to touch it to see if it'd crunch. You pressed my hand against your face.

When we got to Julian, we had mussed hair and squinty eyes. We followed signs directing us to berries, apples, and cherries.

Once we got the white box back into the car I cut the red and white string with my incisors.

Stoned and elated we ate the pie with our hands. In silence we smiled through fistfuls of cherry crumble, mouths in mechanical motion. Red dyed our hands and lips while our nails scraped the bottom of the metal tin.

Your mouth full you said, "I love you so fucking much it's freaking me out," and pastry crust decorated your chin.

"Me or the pie?"

You shrugged, and we laughed, and the syrupy treacle sweetness poured down my throat.

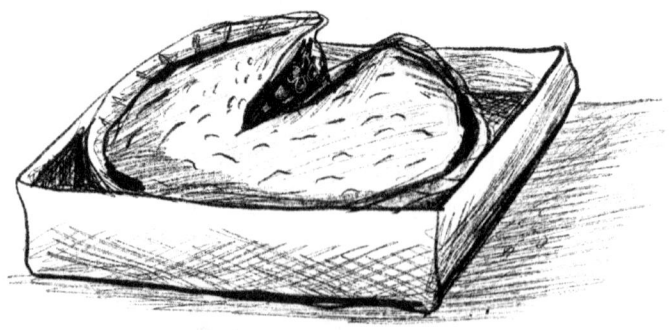

La Felicità

When you and I went camping we accidentally erected the tent near a nest of wasps, or were they yellow jackets? Our camping kinesis unleashed the mustard bodies of floating stingers that lived in a hollowed-out base of a rotting tree. We took shelter twenty feet away, leaving the angry yellow cloud to their stump. Insects in summertime Maryland were angrier than we'd imagined.

In the shade of the nylon, we shared a joint while sweat beaded on our bare limbs – droplets caught in the date-colored hair of your arms. Your body smelled like a ripe fig. Camping dilettantes, we rustled through our plastic bag of snacks looking for tepid bottles of water to quench the thirst that came with the end of summer fog. Dressed in only underwear, we unzipped the mouth of the tent in the hopes a nonexistent breeze would cool us down.

The land below the camp was bouncy with damp grass and the smudge of muddy, rain-bloated earth. We poked our living room floor and watched the below-us-perspiration splotch at our touch.

The cicadas hummed in swells as the evening fell; I told you I wanted to live in the tent forever. Our thighs touched as we surveyed our domicile. I suggested we name our new home like elegant people did in olden days. *La Felicità.*

While you slept, I admired the perspiration that stained your forehead. As I looked at you, I tried to find a word that meant "love" but was not "love" – a word that people chomp on too often, turning the syllables into beige gum. Our mansion-tent swayed in the firefly nighttime, and I fell into dreamlessness thinking about how *this* existed before you and it exists now with you. The wordless feeling is the same as the old feeling, but somehow not the same at all.

Publix Fried Chicken

Rituals and reassurances are like a weathervane. And I love you like the way that people love Cheddar Bay biscuits – how that's a *thing*, like when you go to Red Lobster just for them. Or the way I can only really eat a meal when I'm re-watching a movie I like. Your right palm has an extra-long life line and there is no place I wouldn't follow it.

One time on a road trip, you pulled me inside a Publix and said that it had the world's best fried chicken. I had never heard of Publix before but I was dazzled by how bright it was inside, brighter than the Hadron Collider with all of those particles and are they aiming for time travel there?
The scent inside Publix was a time machine.

The smell reminded me of sterilized fast food like that McDonald's inside Scripps Children's Hospital where I worked as a volunteer as a sixteen-year-old until I was fired (can you be fired when you're a volunteer?). I used to sneak Chicken McNugget meals before going home for dinner, six piece / then ten / and one time a twenty piece and I got so sick when I had to eat dinner later that twenty piece night.

My whole world spun in the Publix and we were a whirligig; love is like that with all the spinning. When I was in first grade, all the kids were outside for recess and Dan told me that if you spun as fast as you could and laid on the ground you'd travel to a different dimension. So I moved like a top across the gravel with my skirt like a bell.

Children are filled with so much music.

I don't know if I've ever returned from that schoolyard alternate dimension and maybe I'm wedged in a world filled with spirals. But whether I am or I'm not, I'm glad that I get to live life in a circle with you in the bright brightness of Publix.

You decided on a mixed eight piece and each were individual laughing golden suns. Medallions / doubloons / treasure in a windowed bucket like a little home and I knew you knew that I would love this. Faces are measured in plans and programming, and yours is charted and diagrammed with times spent in vehicles seeking out and capturing lost feelings from childhood memories.

We moved out of the sun star of the Publix and sat in your silver Honda that you called the Femme Bot. And we ate our pieces, drumstick for me and breast for you. The different patterns of the Publix fried chicken's taste and texture made a quilt of memory for the afternoon. The grease leaked through the box and made a map on my jeans and the constellation patterns were oily hydrogen and helium guiding us. You squinted at the sun with a slick shine around your lips that looked like the lip gloss kids wear when they first get into makeup. Lines from a life well-lived creased near your eyes.

We ate our fill and still had one more piece left, fried chicken that kept on giving. You turned the key when we were done and said, "Not bad, huh?"

I love you like the way food is good and Publix is bright and how the leftover chicken became the topper for a salad the next day, everything all wilted from too much time in the car – us too. You and I live in an alternate universe with so many rotations, and we're dizzily driving in circles using the map of specks on my jeans and the diagrammed history in your hands to move us back and forth through time. "No, not bad. Not bad at all."

There was No Salt in the House

We sat at our kitchen table with the stained blue tablecloth we thought would class up our empty apartment. The light from our trash-picked lamp cast shadows across your face and you looked like a dusty blue-eyed painting. Our table sat next to a window in the living room with the Venetian blinds torn off, and you were a part of the atmosphere.

During that endless summer, there was no salt in the house, so I flavored our meals with the rust from the bumper of your old Buick Le Sabre. We had made a promise that no matter how drunk we got, we'd never get dinner from 7-11 on 40th and Walnut again. Two weeks later, we broke the promise and giggled like little kids going against the adult us-es as we swayingly pointed out what we wanted to eat, little foam mustaches of porter on our faces. Twin conspirators, we picked out some extra bags of Lay's potato chips – salt and vinegar and sour cream and onion – and laughed the entirety of the two blocks home. Your face was covered in blonde crumbs.

We had, and still have, no condiments and a salt fiend and a hot sauce addict need their tools for the beer blunted blandness of 7-11 meals. I tried to wipe the crumbs from your face, a potato-y seasoning, and you wondered aloud in your scratchy voice why no one had marketed potato pepper yet.

Pulling from somewhere in our boozey brains, we started talking about chemistry classes from high school and how salt was made. How it's a chemical and a mineral – plant, animal, air, earth – pool water and ocean waves. We figured salt was found in everything, the heated film of our skins, soda cups, chairs. Everything. We'd just need to grate the substance from any surface. I licked a portion of my damp sweating arm – salt all around us. You rubbed your hand against the stubble on your jaw and it sounded like a cat purring, somewhere outside a car alarm

went off and you made an Abbott Costello face at the sound. We both looked outside at the street.

Rust is corrosion and oxidation. It's iron oxide formed on either iron or steel. And we both knew that your old golden LeSabre was a breeding ground for that tarnished spice. Your bumper was the paprika of salt. When I drew the grater across it, rust fell like rain into a white porcelain bowl, damaged from its prior life in a thrift store and its life even before that. We loved that bowl for its imperfection, grinning at us with its chipped tooth body. Your car was our spice vessel and I filled the bowl with a layer of the flaking LeSabre. The humidity caused sweat to pour from our armpits, and the beer mustaches were mixed with the salty dampness of our bodies. Before we took the bowl back inside, you slapped the hood of the LeSabre and I gently touched my lips to its gilded body.

Your car was in our meals that night and we became part machine. We moved mouths around our drunk repast, our gingered supper, and we were salt and earth and air and water and animal and that one road trip in a beat up car from Philly to Chester to see if we could find original recipe Four Lokos. There is no salt in rust, but we flavored our food with it anyway. Wily demons fucking around for the fun of it, you distributed another spoonful of reddishness across your pizza like the way my mother would spoon Parmesan cheese across her lasagna.

The light from the lamp still shone on you, and after eating I kissed the intermingled dark and light shades from your face. The aging of machinery fresh in our mouths. We were both machines and imperfect chipped china bowls once loved in different lifetimes. Across the table from one another, high school chemistry having failed us, I could still taste the salt from your skin, the freshness of your flesh better than any meal I've ever eaten.

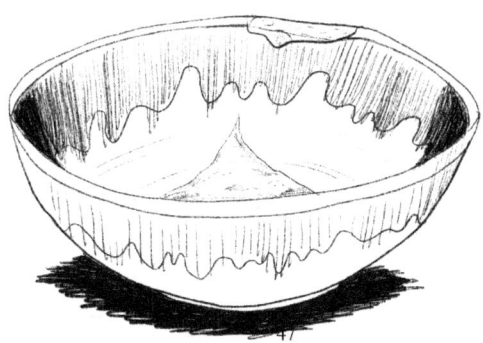

Anthropophagus Means Cannibal or Man-Eater

My desire is a cannibal. It's a tiger standing on train
tracks with the baying of the air horn begging
me away. I'm a rickety overpass and my longing is a compass
driving me toward open bodies with split apart ribcages and I want to
live inside of them. This guy and I are cannibals connected to bodies
functioning off of remorse – "no thanks, I don't want any of your
melted ice cream," I say as we bump knees on
his bed that's also a couch watching X-Files
together. I'd prefer him to stop rustling his own hair and rhapsodizing
the grandeur of his awesome self, I mean he's no
Fox Mulder, after all. But I'm flesh and he's flesh and the
meat of my mouth is going to drain him, and it does.
I'm an entire person who eats others to fill
my insides. I'd like to chew on the bits of his
body where decency lives, maybe on the inside?, but I'll still settle on
the outside parts. If he ate the inside parts
of me, he'd find hidden stuff like how I'm an adult
but, like a kid, I'll hold onto my
old stuffed animal and cry sometimes.
It's hard to be a lonely grown-up kid and a cannibal at the same time.
And this guy would be able to see that with 1st bite; he's
an emotional wendigo – but not so keen on me. I do
all the eating, and after we fall asleep on the bed-couch
in the cadaver yellow light of a late night / early AM. When I go to examine
my face upon waking, I like the way I look having fallen asleep with a wet face
and makeup still on. I stand silently at his sink while he's asleep, in
the mirror my face is tracked with acid rain. I'm a
golden mystic of 2 AM tater tots – devouring them with
the blood of strange boys in strange homes. Hungriness is like how prophets
saw the prophecies in the smoke of poison fires. In the home of this
also-cannibal's, I
can guess the man-eating-mistakes awaiting us in future fires.
The previous past is painted on my morning cheeks,
my cheeks are apples under
stretched freckles. I wish the boy in the bed would

take a big bite out of them and then we could
be fortune telling flesh eaters together. But cannibals can't also
be carcasses and seeing beyond sight isn't for duo man-eaters.
Before I leave, I study his sleeping body – a steak in a case –
the sheet is a skin shedder – a reptile molting.
Shifted off his shoulder blades – they're sharp
as spears. I could pick the meat out of my teeth with
his daggery collarbones. Maybe modern-day monsters can't sync
like phones. So, I become a blank screen leaving as
a shell having digested what I came for – or what I thought I came
for. In wakefulness, he won't remember me. We are concomitant
beasts bleeding out these brief memories – together but apart.
Lonesome miseries, never stuffed.
Cars pass, but none are mine, I shift my feet and wait for
my getaway outside the butcher shop of the boy's apartment. The wind lifts
my skirt like the sheets that you raise up into
sails – full blown. My body, forever hungry and next meal awaiting,
looks like a mailbox full of love letters.

Acknowledgements

"Fighting Over the Best Flavor in Neapolitan Ice Cream" and *La Felicità*" were published by *Crack the Spine*; "Three AM, February 26th," was published by *Bull: Men's Fiction*; "My 1st Crush is Getting Married" was published by *Sweet Tree Review*; "How to Break a Haymaker" was published by *#thesideshow* (part of *Five 2 One Magazine*); "Water out of Wine Glasses" was published by *Bending Genres*; "The Washing Machine Sang" was published by *South Broadway Ghost Society*; "Building Bodies" was published by *Soft Cartel*; "Saint Day" was published by *Taco Bell Review*; "Lodestar, South Carolina" was published by *Dirty Chai Magazine*; "Falling Toast" was published by *Ghost Parachute*; "I wanted us to be French Impressionists" was published by *Right Hand Pointing*; "Consider Ravioli" was published by *X-Ray Lit*; "Julian, CA" was published by *Black Heart Magazine*; "Lexical gustatory synesthesia" was published by *Whiskey Paper* Review; "Publix Fried Chicken" was published by *Secret History Books*; "There was no salt in the house" was published by *Empty House Press*; "Anthropophagus means cannibal or man-eater" was published by *Horror Sleaze Trash*

www.ingramcontent.com/pod-product-compliance
Lightning Source LLC
Chambersburg PA
CBHW060749210726
48292CB00015B/2888